ERIC!

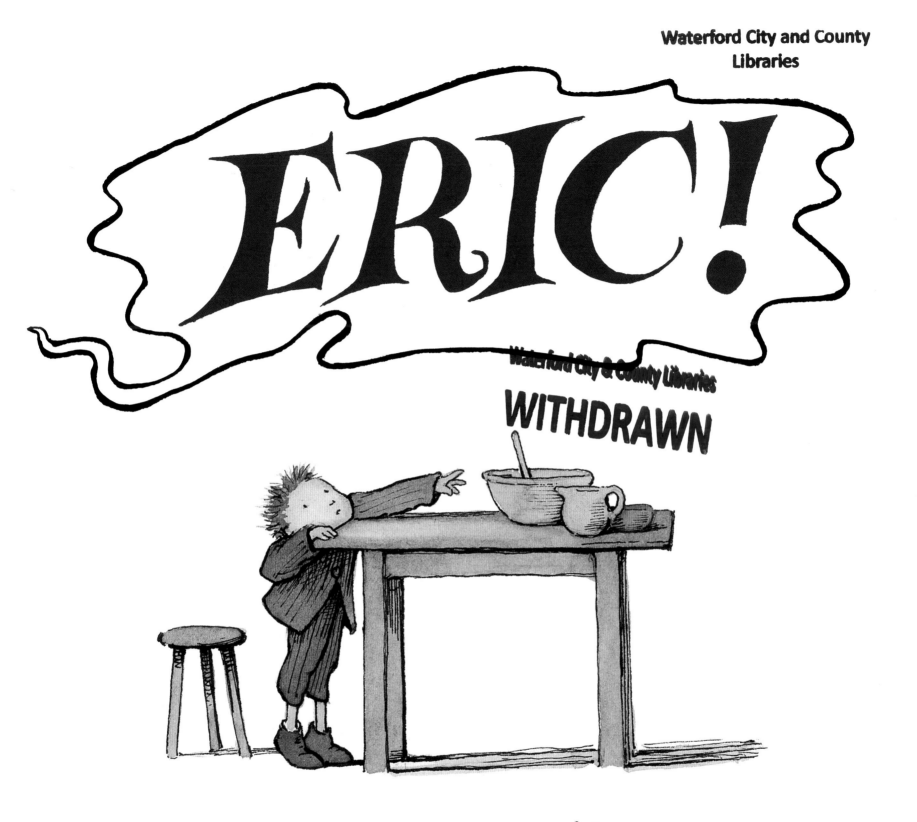

Chris Wormell

A Tom Maschler Book
Jonathan Cape • London

Have you ever done something stupid? I'm sure you have. I know I have; I've done lots of stupid things. And I've been called all kinds of names. I've been called a nit and a twerp and a dimwit. But I don't think I was ever that stupid. I may be a bit slow sometimes, and clumsy too, and there are lots of things I'm not very good at. But you can't be good at everything. And it sometimes takes a while to find out what you are good at. It did with me.

This is the story of Eric, who was a little bit like me.

He seemed to be no good at anything, and was called so many names he came to believe that he really was a

And a

I know exactly how he felt.

There have been days when it seemed that I hadn't a single friend, and that no one in the whole wide world cared much about me. Well, so it was with Eric.

One day he felt so miserable, he ran away. And he wasn't even very good at that – the running part, at least; he soon grew tired and began to walk.

He was dawdling along, swishing a stick at the wayside nettles and kicking at stones in the path, when all of a sudden he heard a shout . . .

came the cry from somewhere up ahead.

RUN FOR YOUR LIVES!
A HUGE MONSTER HAS COME
DOWN FROM THE MOUNTAINS!

A woodcutter came rushing out of the wood. And suddenly, all around, people began to run for their lives, fleeing across the fields towards the castle of the king.

Eric turned and ran with them.

And as the people ran, they felt the ground shake, and they heard the STOMP! STOMP! STOMP! of the monster's enormous steps. And they all ran faster . . .

But Eric stopped . . . and thought:

I'm a TWIT. And a NITWIT and a DUMMY and a DUNCE and a DOPE . . . Perhaps I'm a hero? Perhaps that's what I'm good at?

And because he was never afraid to try anything, he turned and stood there, waiting for the monster.

And the STOMP! STOMP! STOMP! of the monster's steps grew louder and louder.

And all the people ran faster and faster until at last they reached the castle of the king. And when they were safely inside and the drawbridge was pulled up and they were all watching from the battlements, the king said . . .

Who's that down there?

And everybody looked and saw a little figure standing all alone. And they said,

What does he think he's doing? The TWIT!

But it *was* too late. For there was the monster, crashing through the wood, smashing at the trees with an uprooted trunk and crunching rocks and boulders with his great stomping feet. On and on he came – STOMP! STOMP! STOMP! – until he spied a little figure standing all alone. Then he stopped, and looked down at Eric. And Eric looked up at the monster, and said . . .

And then something very strange happened. The monster
looked ever so sad, and said in a deep mournful voice,

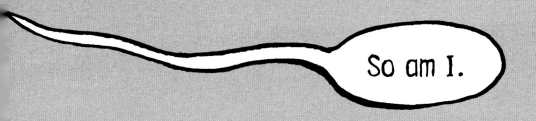

So am I.

And he laid down the uprooted tree trunk and sat down
with a great sigh, and said . . .

At least, that's what all the other monsters say.
I'm no good at anything. I can't flatten a mountain
with my fist. I can't howl at the moon and make
the stars tremble – I can't even swallow a
grizzly bear whole! I'm a hopeless monster, and all
the others laugh at me. So I ran away and came
down here. And I wonder if there is anyone
in the whole wide world who cares. I don't think
I have a single friend.

A great tear welled up in the
monster's eye, then fell with a splash.

Eric stepped over the puddle, went right up
to the monster and gave his foot a little pat.
He said,

I'll be your friend.

Will you?

replied the monster.

Yes, I will. And I think you're a brilliant monster! You really scared everybody around here – they all ran for their lives!

Did they?

Yes, they did! And now they're all hiding in that castle over there.

Are they? Oh dear, I didn't really mean to scare them. I didn't scare you, did I?

Eric shook his head.

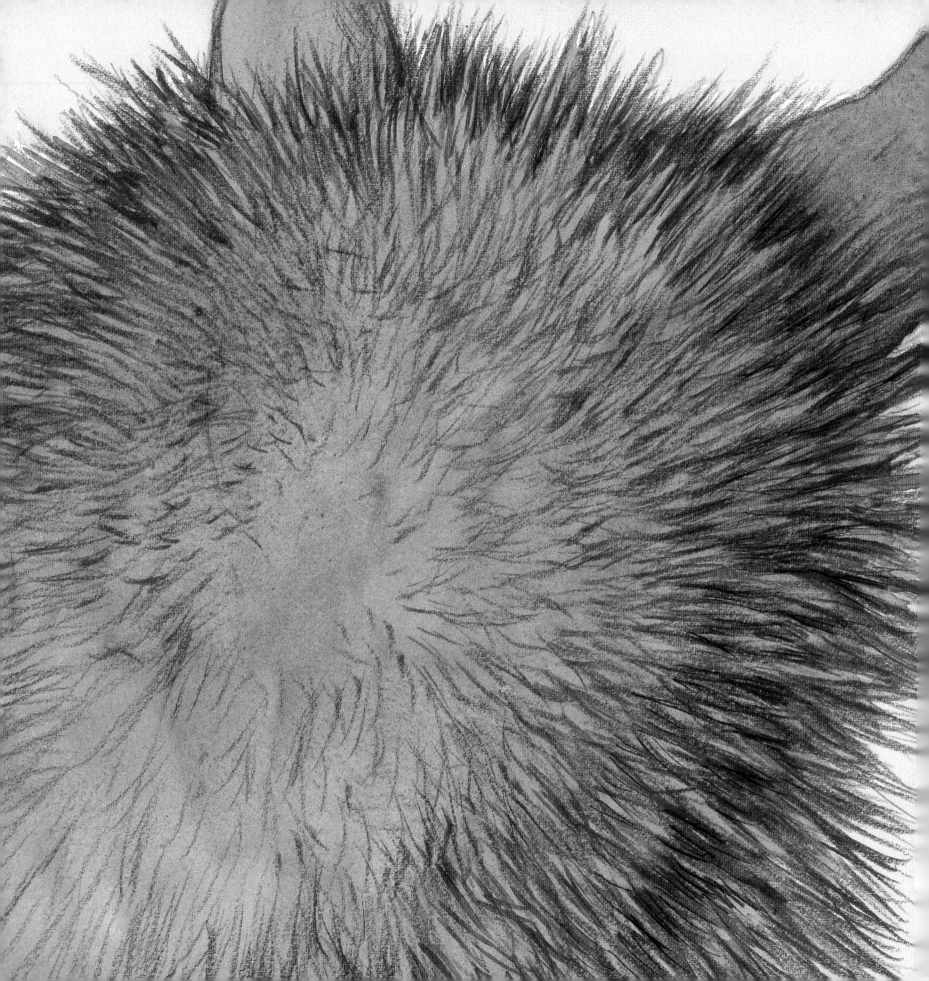

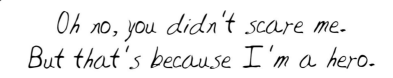

And do you know what?

Everybody agreed – he was!

For Julia

ERIC!
A JONATHAN CAPE BOOK 978 0 224 08396 6

Published in Great Britain by Jonathan Cape,
an imprint of Random House Children's Books
A Random House Group Company

This edition published 2012

3 5 7 9 10 8 6 4 2

RANDOM HOUSE CHILDREN'S BOOKS
61–63 Uxbridge Road, London W5 5SA

www.**kids**at**randomhouse**.co.uk
www.**randomhouse**.co.uk

Addresses for companies within The Random House Group Limited can be found at:
www.randomhouse.co.uk/offices.htm

THE RANDOM HOUSE GROUP Limited Reg. No. 954009

A CIP catalogue record for this book is available from the British Library.

Printed and bound in China